S0-AFD-364

NORMAN BRIDWELL

Clifford's
FIRST HALLOWEEN

SCHOLASTIC INC.
New York   Toronto   London   Auckland   Sydney

For Alissa Bridwell Merz

ISBN 0-590-50317-0

Copyright © 1995 by Norman Bridwell.
All rights reserved. Published by Scholastic Inc.
CLIFFORD and the CLIFFORD logo are registered trademarks of Norman Bridwell.

25 24 23 22 21 20   1 2 3 4

Printed in the U.S.A.   23

First Scholastic printing, September 1995
Colorist: Manny Campana

Trick or treat! I'm Emily Elizabeth, the cat,
and the BIG red clown is my dog, Clifford.
Clifford was not always this big.

Many Halloweens ago, he was just a tiny red puppy.

I wanted to take Clifford out trick-or-treating.
But the mask and hat didn't fit.
He was not a happy clown.

I tried dressing him as an angel.

While I was putting my fairy costume on,
he ate his halo.

Then I found the perfect costume
for my small red puppy.

Clifford was the littlest ghost I had ever seen.

My neighbors were nice.

We both got lots of good treats.

When we got home, Daddy was carving a pumpkin for our Halloween party.

Clifford was a nosy little puppy.

Now we had a jack-o'-lantern that barked and stuck out its tongue.

I showed Clifford my Halloween noisemaker.

He was surprised.

Then it was time for the party.
All my friends came.

Mommy made us candy apples.

Clifford wondered how they tasted.

The candy was sort of sticky.

I had to give Clifford a quick bath.

It was time to go into the haunted house.
Our jack-o'-lantern looked very spooky.

Clifford followed me into the haunted house.

But he didn't like it very much.

Then Mommy dimmed the lights and told a scary story about a haunted hand that crept around the house.

Suddenly we all saw a giant hand wriggling on the wall.
We were scared!

What was it?

The hand came closer and closer.

We laughed when we saw it was only Clifford.

It was a great party.

Clifford is grown up now, but he still makes Halloween
a special day for everyone.